WEST TO FREEDOM
a story of friendship

written by
J. Arthur Moore

Omnibook Co. New York, New York

Printed in New York by:

OMNIBOOK CO.
99 Wall Street, Suite 118
New York, NY 10005
USA
+1-866-216-99652
www.omnibookcompany.com

For e-book purchase: Kindle on Amazon, Barnes and Noble
Wholesale purchase: Ingram (615) 793-5000,
Baker & Taylor (800) 775-1800
Book purchase: Amazon.com, Barnes & Noble.com, www.jarthurmoore.com
and www.omnibookcompany.com/journeyintodarkness/

Omnibook titles may be purchased in bulk for educational, business, fund-raising, or sales promotional use. For more information please e-mail info@omnibookcompany.com

DEDICATION

West to Freedom is dedicated in His love and in friendship to Thomas Ristine and John Rivera who have helped bring the characters of the story to life by representing them with their images, and to all who share in reading this adventure in friendship.

THOMAS REYNOLDS

Daniel Russell

Thomas and Daniel had been the best of friends all their lives. They had grown up together on the waterfront of the small town of Ozark, Arkansas, on the western reaches of the Arkansas River. Thomas Reynolds was a cabin boy on the riverboat Ozark Queen, having grown up in Ozark where his father ran a freight business. Daniel Russell, a slave by birth, had been sold as a baby off a plantation in Mississippi and purchased by George Morton, a kindly businessman who was traveling on his way to take over a general store in Ozark. Since the two men were business associates, their babies were frequently together as their wives attended the same small country church and worked together on various social projects. As toddlers, the boys would play together. As they grew, they often helped out at the two businesses, doing odd jobs and running errands. The fact that one was white and the other was mulatto never bothered them as young children. But now that they were in their thirteenth year, it had become obvious. Daniel was not allowed to go to school with Thomas, nor was he permitted many freedoms that Thomas took for granted. Thomas and Daniel both became increasingly aware of the restrictions on the colored youth, no matter that he could pass for white, and the fact that he only enjoyed the kindness of Mr. Morton as long as he was owned by the man, for he was a kind master who cared about Daniel's welfare. Thomas had become a cabin boy when he was ten years old. His father had decided that it would be good for his son to see more of the world and be exposed to a greater variety of opportunities as he traveled the river. For the past two years, the two saw less of each other and looked forward to every stop the Ozark Queen made at Ozark.

*　　*　　*

It was a brilliant spring morning in mid April 1862 as the *Queen* approached the wharves of Ozark. Twelve-year-old Thomas was in the pilot house gathering together Captain Kearny's papers including shipping orders, maps, and newspapers, while the captain carefully guided his pilot as the young man steered the boat toward the docks.

"Reverse engines!" the captain called through the speaking tube to the engine room below. "Soft to port, Teddy," he instructed his pilot. There was a soft scraping sound as the right side of the riverboat slid along the wharf. "Secure the lines!" Kearney called to the deck hands. "Run out the gang plank!" he ordered.

Within minutes the *Ozark Queen* was tied against the dock and the gangway was run out. The noise of arrival shifted to a loud orderly chaos as passengers departed the boat and work crews began to unload cargo from the freight deck.

The boy of slender build stood nearly five feet tall. Hazel eyes concentrated through wire-rimmed glasses as he placed the captain's papers in a leather case and took them to Captain Kearney by the deck railing outside the pilot house where he was shouting instructions to the crew below.

"Will there be anything else, Captain?" the boy asked

"That's all for now, Thomas. Run along, now, but be sure to be back by noon tomorrow to prepare to leave for the trip back south." The captain placed his hands on the boy's shoulders. "Thanks for your assistance. Enjoy your time off."

Captain Kearny took the case from Thomas's hands and waved him off.

*   *   *

"Daniel" Thomas called as he burst through the door into the Morton General Store. He paused to allow his eyes to adjust to the dark interior of the store. "There was a battle in Tennessee last Sunday and Monday!" He found his friend at the counter in the back of the store. "Thousands were killed! This war's really gonna be bad!"

"Let me finish here first, Thomas," Daniel replied.

There were a few moments of quiet while the young, dark-skinned clerk with long black hair tied up in a bun, finished with his customer. The woman took her packages and left.

"What else have you heard?" Daniel asked. He walked around from the back side of the counter to join his friend. "Sit here." he offered.

The two, Thomas the taller of the two, met at several unopened crates from the morning delivery and chose places to sit.

"Many on the boat are talking about slaves and how they need to be better controlled so they don't run away or join with the abolitionists who are killing slave owners and anyone else they might think favors slave-owning. One man told of how he beats his slaves regularly so that they'll know who's boss and not even think about running. I sure am glad Mr. Morton owns you. He's 'bout the nicest slave owner I know."

"You're right, of course. But I'm real worried. Business ain't goin' so well and there's been talk that he might loose everything to the bank. And you know old Nabors; he'd sell anything that would bring him a dollar." Daniel was worried. He looked at his friend and there was fear in his dark eyes.

"We're gonna have to figure a way to get you out of here to somewhere where you'll be safe, forever." Thomas stated.

"But how can we do that and where can I go?" Daniel worried.

"I'm not sure. But my pa really cares about you and about Mr. Morton. I'll talk to him tonight and see if he has any ideas."

The boys walked around to the store counter where the jar of peppermint sticks awaited any who were offered. Each took one then wandered toward the front door.

"What do you hear from your ma?" Daniel asked.

"Her last letter said Grandpa is slowly recovering from his heart attack. But she doesn't expect to return for at least another month," Thomas replied. He paused to enjoy the candy.

"I'm supposed to be back on the Queen by noon tomorrow to leave south again," Thomas informed. "So why don't you see if you can come over to the freight office after breakfast and help out some. Maybe I'll have something by then"

"Okay," Daniel replied, "I'm sure it'll be okay by Mr. Morton."

The boys stood inside the door sucking for a while on their candy. Neither spoke for several minutes.

"See you then," Thomas said. Then he stepped into the sunlight and turned toward the freight office and home.

*　　*　　*

The sun was just beginning to rise on the new day, casting long low beams of light through the windows in the front of the freight company's office. The business consisted of a collection of buildings with an enclosed yard area within. The office was in front. Beside it a gate opened into the yard which was surrounded with the stables, warehouses, wagon sheds and a residence, all located behind the office building which had rooms on the second floor for employees who lived on the premises. Only a clerk remained of the many who had worked there, since many had left to serve in the war.

Soft footsteps crossed the wooden porch outside and approached the office door. It squeaked open as Daniel entered and paused for his eyes to adjust to the dimness of the office interior.

"Hey," Thomas greeted as he entered from the back room.

"Any ideas?" Daniel asked as he found a chair near the office desk.

Thomas pulled up a chair and began to share a plan his father had worked out the previous night. "Pa will tell Captain Kearney that he needs me for several weeks to drive shipments to western forts, since most of his men had to leave to join the army. This is how you fit in."

Thomas explained the plan. He would be driving a shipment of dry goods to Fort Wayne in the eastern part of the Oklahoma territory, not far from the northwest corner of Arkansas. His pa would tell Mr. Morton that he needs to rent Daniel's services to help drive a wagon since he no longer had any drivers because of the war, and Thomas would not be able to drive both wagons that were needed to make the deliveries. The boys would work out a plan so that Thomas could report that Daniel was lost for some reason and didn't make it back.

"How will we do that?" Daniel asked excitedly.

"I haven't worked that out yet," Thomas replied, "But I'm sure we'll come up with a really good story. Pa's goin' to see Mr. Morton now and to work out a rent agreement and pay him for your services. Right now, we gotta pack some clothes, food, blankets, and provisions for us on the trip. When Pa gets back, we gotta load the wagons and get the horses ready for tomorrow."

The boys went to Thomas's room and started by putting together an extra set of clothes for each. Moving back to the office and work area, they searched out a haversack for each in which to pack his things. Rain gear and coats were taken down from coat racks. Thomas took a case of cartridges and boxes of caps for his revolver and took down a cartridge bag, cap pouch, and holster. Taking three spare cylinders from the store shelves, Thomas motioned for Daniel to join him at a work table where they found stools to sit down and load the revolver and its cylinders. Before starting to work, Thomas laid out all his materials, then went back to the store shelves to pick out all the same for Daniel.

"Daniel," Thomas instructed, "watch what I do and you do the same."

Thomas pulled the hammer to half cock. Then he took a cartridge, put the powder into a chamber, put the ball on top, lined up the chamber with the built in ram, and rammed the load tight into the chamber. Daniel did the same with his revolver with help from his friend. The process was repeated until the chambers were fully loaded. Next, the cylinders were removed from the guns, replaced with one of the empty ones in each, and the loading process repeated. Finally, the last cylinder was loaded. A brass cap was placed on the nipple of each chamber for each cylinder. When all was completed, Thomas lit a beeswax candle and sealed every chamber and nipple to protect from dampness, water, weather. The guns were ready. They were placed in their holsters and the cylinders placed in the cartridge pouches along with extra cartridges.

"Thanks." Daniel stated when they had finished. "That sure was a lot of work."

"It pays to have the spares ready so that you don't have to reload in the middle of a fight. All you have to do is change out cylinders."

The office door opened and Mr. Reynolds strode into the room. He was a large, heavy-set man, in his early forties, balding on top, his skin weathered from years of driving wagon and exposure to the weather and its changes. Crossing the room in long even strides, he stopped beside the boys and observed their work as they packed the revolvers into individual haversacks.

"They loaded and ready?" the man asked.

"Done, Pa," Thomas replied.

"What about a couple of rifled muskets?" Mr. Reynolds offered.

"They might come in handy," the son agreed.

"Load six and pack a case of ammunition." He selected six rifles and lay them out on the work table while the boys brought out a case of cartridges and set them on the floor beside the work area.

The three worked together to load all six weapons, then set them aside with the growing collection of personal supplies.

"Come, sit and have a cup of coffee while I explain the plan I have put together for you two." Mr. Reynolds led the way to the stove where the pot of coffee sat and kept warm. "Here," he offered as he filled a tin cup for each. "Pull up chairs to the desk."

All gathered around the office desk and sat sipping their cups of coffee while Thomas's pa explained the plan he had put together. For a moment Thomas's glasses steamed up from the vapor off the hot coffee. Taking a bandana from his back pocket, he wiped them clean and readjusted them on his face, pushing them back up on the bridge of his nose with his finger.

"Thomas, I've spoken to Captain Kearney and he is okay working this trip without ya. Daniel, I've spoken to Mr. Morton. You are officially paid for, rented and working for me. I've told him no more, but I think he suspects and is hopeful for your freedom. He won't say. He can't say for your sake as well as for his.

"We will pack the wagons today and you will leave early tomorrow morning. There will be two wagons. I have some Cherokee friends in the camp outside the fort and am sending some blankets and food supplies for their people. There will also be some weapons for hunting and pots and tools for the women. One blanket will have a letter for a warrior named Runs Like the

Wind. I don't want you to carry it in case you are stopped. You will carry a copy of the agreement to rent Daniel's services. That way, no one can say you knew anything. The letter explains that Daniel needs to get free because his master, who has been kind to him, is in financial trouble and might loose him; could he be adopted into the tribe and become a Cherokee. But act as though he was kidnapped and stolen by the Indians. When you give the blanket to Runs Like the Wind, explain about the letter and ask him to burn it after he has read it. This way Daniel will be free, but no one will know that it was planned.

"Does that sound okay to you boys?" the man asked.

"Wow!" Thomas exclaimed.

"That's some plan!" Daniel put in. "This Cherokee warrior must be someone special."

"He is," Mr. Reynolds confirmed. "I've known him for many years. We met when I was out hunting buffalo for the army and a band of Cherokee attacked me. I offered my weapon, butt first, to the lead warrior as a sign of respect. It was Runs Like the Wind and he responded with respect, ordering those with him to not shoot. We went back to their camp. He explained with broken English that I was trespassing on tribal hunting lands. I explained that I was only hunting meat for the soldiers and did not plan to take any more than I could carry. He suggested that I should pay for taking from their lands and I offered my buffalo gun in exchange for the meat I was taking. The trade was accepted and we parted friends. Since then I have sent an occasional wagon load of goods and kept a friendly association with him and his people. Once, when he was younger, I took Thomas on a trip and Runs Like the Wind accepted him right away as a friend of the

Cherokee. He even said that when he was of age, he could go on his vision quest and become an adopted warrior with his band. Thomas, this is your thirteenth summer. It is time if you wish to accept."

"Golly!" Daniel whispered.

"I don't know," Thomas added. "I don't know that much about his customs and this vision quest."

"Don't worry about it now." Mr. Reynolds stood and gathered up the set of papers from a pile on his desk. "Let's get this load on the wagons and pack your gear. You have a long journey ahead of you in the morning."

The three proceeded to pull the goods from the warehouse and to pack the wagons. The man had great strength from years of strenuous work. The boys, both slender build, likewise had unexpected strength in solid muscles, from their youthful years of hard work. There were cases of dry goods in food, both boxed and canned. Bolts of cloth were added for the trading post for the women moving west in the wagon trains. Tools, hardware, nails, screws, rolls of barbed wire, and cut glass were put in for those who were in need to help build new homes. Kitchen ware and blankets and a number of trade goods such as beads and small knives were added to a part of the load destined for the Indian people. Some guns and cases of ammunition were tucked in under the rest of the load. Some were for the trading store and some were for Runs Like the Wind's people. One wagon had the camp gear, food, personal equipment, weapons and packs belonging to the boys. Both wagons were equipped with hoop and canvass covers to protect against the weather. One had a tool box on the side and the other a kitchen box. Each had a sling of leather strapping beneath for carrying firewood to be picked up along the way. Each would be pulled by a four-horse hitch and have a saddle horse tied on the back. Saddles and tack would be carried in the wagon with the boy's personal gear and supplies. It was time for supper by the time all was packed and ready. The horses were tied in the stable with extra grain for the long travel that lay ahead. Extra feed was loaded in the wagon with the saddles, but most feeding would be by foraging the grasslands along the way. The wagons waited in the yard area behind the office and warehouse. All was in readiness. Following supper, the boys laid out their clothes before gathering in front of the fireplace in the residence to enjoy some quiet time together and talk about the adventure that lay ahead. Then it was off to bed and a good night's sleep for the day ahead.

*   *   *

Beams of sunlight drifted in through the eastern windows of Thomas's bedroom, alive with a million small particles of dust dancing in their brightness. Daniel stirred in his blanket roll on the spare cot, which squeaked as he shifted to a sitting position. Thomas lay awake in his bed, stretching sleepy muscles as he pushed aside his blanket.

"Guess we might as well get to," Thomas said sleepily.

"Yeh," Daniel agreed. "Hey, that smells good!" he noticed the aroma of breakfast sausages and hotcakes from the kitchen below.

"Pa's already fixin' fer us ta be gettin' ready and on the road." Thomas sat up.

Clothes were already laid out. Daniel pulled on his tan pants, brown store bought shirt, leather vest, and boots. Thomas wore his store-bought clothes including light brown pants, a brown shirt, and boots. He also pulled on buckskin leggings, which he usually wore when driving the wilderness roads. Each grabbed his hat and they clopped down the steps to the kitchen, where the aroma of breakfast cooking blended with the smell of fresh-brewed coffee.

"Mornin', Pa," Thomas greeted.

"Sher smells good," Daniel complimented.

"Mornin', Boys," Mr. Reynolds acknowledged. "Glad you're up to an early start. Town's not yet awake and I hope to beat that and get you on your way before there's any movement about. Pull up yer chairs and grab somethin' ta eat."

Breakfast was eaten without conversation. Each knew what had to be done in order to get under way as quickly as possible. Arising from the table, the boys grabbed their coats, long dusters with cape-like collar and reaching to the tops of their boots, and a pair of leather gloves, then jammed their broad-brimmed hats on their heads and turned toward the door leading to the freight yard.

The teams were led from the stables, harnessed, and hitched to the wagons, The saddle horses were bridled, led to the wagons, and tied to the tail gates. All was ready.

"Keep your weapons under your seats and close by," Mr. Reynolds warned. "There's no tellin' what you'll run into. Feelin's is runnin' high an' divided. There was fightin' up north ta Elkhorn

Tavern last month when Yank forces came down from Missouri. The Southern forces were driven off. At present, Confederate forces are in control at Fort Wayne. But that could change any time. You've a hundred miles ta cross on rough roads an wilderness near the end. Make smart decisions as ya go, and be careful. Take no chances and trust no one."

Everything was done. The boys were ready to leave. Mr. Reynolds reached out to each and embraced each in a warm hug.

"I love ya both. God, I hope yer trip is safe. Now be off. Remember, north ta Cass an stay over with the Keltons. Then it's north toward St. Paul taking the northwest fork to Fayetteville. You'll spend the night along the road, pick a safe spot well off the road and out of sight, and no fire. Stay at Morgan's in Fayetteville; then north to Bentonville where you'll stay with Sheriff Carleton. From there it's cross country following the river to Fort Wayne. Stop outside the fort first to look up Runs Like the Wind. When finished there, go on to the trading post inside the fort. From there make your own best decisions. If need, sell a wagon and pack all your gear into the other for the return trip. Or sell both and keep horses as pack animals to carry your gear coming back. Thomas, you will probably need both saddle horses for the return trip in case you need to move more quickly. Whatever decisions you make, I trust you to make whatever is right for the situation. It's time ta go."

The boys climbed up to their respective wagon seats and settled in to move out. Mr. Reynolds walked over to the yard's gate and swung it wide for the wagons to pass. Taking up the reins, each boy slapped his team into motion and guided his wagon toward the open road. Thomas's pa waved to each as his wagon passed and each waved back.

"Be careful," he offered one last time.

"We will," each replied.

The man watched as the wagons rolled on down the empty street and became lost in the road dust kicked up by wagon wheels and their teams. The jingle of trace chains and the crunch of wagon wheels on dirt and gravel quieted into the distance. The man stood watching until all was quiet and only the distant cloud of trail dust could be seen. Then it, too, faded and he turned to the gateway and swung the gates closed.

*   *   *

The first two days went smoothly according to plan. The Keltons took good care of the boys the first night and saw to it the horses were rested, fed, and cared for. The boys slept under the wagons, ate well, made their visits to the outhouse, and were on their way early the following morning. Just past St. Paul, they pulled onto the road to Fayetteville. By late afternoon, they found some small hills off to the side of the road and drove their wagons into a stand of trees near a small creek. Before setting camp, each took a leafy tree branch and walked back to the road where they backed away toward their wagons, brushing away the wagon tracks as they went. While there was still plenty of sunlight, a small cook fire was lit and they heated each a can of beans, fried up some salt pork, and brewed a pot of coffee. When the cooking was finished, the fire was put out and covered over with dirt. After eating and cleaning up, time was spent gathering firewood and stowing it in the harnessing beneath the wagons. A rope line was set for the horses and they were unhitched, taken to water, then tied to graze for the night. Bedding was laid out beneath a wagon, weapons were placed at the head of each, and the boys settled in for the night.

Up early the next morning, each had a cold cup of coffee and some cold beans from the night before. All was packed, the horses were hitched, and the two were on their way once more, headed first back to the road, then northwest toward Fayetteville. The sun was low at their backs and the road was empty and quiet.

*   *   *

Two hours into the day, the sun was higher and the shadows off the left side of the wagons were shorter. Thomas pulled up his team to rest as Daniel pulled alongside and did the same. Out of habit, the boys surveyed their surroundings for any sign of activity. Far ahead on the horizon a small cloud of dust seemed to be growing. Someone was coming. They waited.

"Put on yer gun," Thomas advised.

Each reached under his seat and drew out his gun belt and cartridge pouch. The gun was buckled on and the pouch slung over the shoulder.

"They're ridin' toward the sun and won't see us good as we'll see them," Thomas commented.

"What now?" his companion asked.

"Let's move on slowly. But be ready to run for it to the rocks on the right where we might be able to fight if need, or at least get to our horses and make a run fer it." Thomas eased back on the reins to slow the team.

"Could we have time to pull off before they see us and wait for them to pass?" Daniel suggested.

"You could be right," Thomas agreed. "Let's do it slowly to keep the dust down and get some branches and cover our tracks."

The boys slowly pulled their wagons off to the side of the road and back as far as they could into the rocks and underbrush. Tying the teams to tree saplings, they broke off a leafy branch each and walked out to carefully sweep away their tracks. They had strapped on their gun belts, slung cartridge pouches over their shoulders, and now took two rifles each, then took up sheltered positions in the rocks. There they waited to let the oncoming riders pass, to observe if they might be friendly or dangerous.

Fifteen minutes seemed forever, but then the sound of approaching horsemen could be heard, moving slowly at an easy gait. There must be more than a dozen riders, Thomas determined as he listened for them to pass and tried to guess a count without peering out and risking being seen.

"Do ya think that cavalry troop is still on our tail?" one asked.

"I tend to doubt it, Jake." another replied. "We should have seen them by now and they would be coming on at a gallop."

"Hey, Tim," another called. "Did you see something up ahead as we crossed the rise back a ways?"

"Not sure," Tim responded. "Could have been the sun playing tricks in this heat. But we should keep an eye out from here on just in case."

"Boys," an authoritative voice spoke up, "St. Paul is a few hours away. Fayetteville is a day's ride behind. So if we do find someone on the road ahead, they should be easy pickings. But remember, if they don't appear to have anything of use, let them pass so we don't stir up possible trouble. But we come upon a wagon of goods, we take it and leave no one to tell. So let's pick up the pace and see if there was something on the road ahead."

The horses picked up speed as the riders urged them on in search of any victims they might find along the way. Soon the sound of galloping hoofs faded into the distance and a quiet settled on the hiding place the boys had chosen.

"Sure am glad we pulled off," Daniel whispered.

"We best wait a spell and give them plenty of time to get on," Thomas stated.

Waiting quietly, the horses grazed on the scrub grass at their feet. The sound of their munching was loud in the silence. Out on the road, the boys watched a rabbit explore the grasses and stop to nibble on some tender looking shoots. Suddenly it scampered off into the underbrush.

"Someone's coming," Thomas warned.

Daniel leaned his two rifles against the rocks beside him, checking to be sure the caps were properly placed. Thomas did the same as each moved to a point where it was possible to watch the road. The wagons were parked with their teams fully hitched and ready to go, in a spot about twenty feet from where the boys watched through the rocks and sapling trees.

As the two watched, the man called Jack along with three of his companions, moved slowly along either side of the road, studying the ground carefully for any sign of tracks.

"Over here," a slender, bearded fellow whispered in a high pitch squeak.

The others joined him as they studied what he had found. The boys pulled back the hammers on their rifles and each picked a target as they waited to see what the four men would do next.

After several minutes of careful study, Jack stood up and pointed toward the place where Thomas and Daniel were hidden. "They can't be far," he said. "Mount up and let's go."

As the four mounted and turned their horses to charge toward the boys, two rifles spoke and two outlaws fell dead.

"Charge," Jack yelled, "before they have time to reload!"

Daniel took aim with his second rifle while Thomas drew his revolver and fired two quick rounds. The men pulled their horses up short and Daniel fired on the closer of the two. He grabbed his arm as his rifle dropped to the ground and turned to get away. Thomas aimed at the last rider, Jack, and squeezed of two more carefully aimed shots. The man slumped forward in the saddle, then fell over to the ground. The remaining rider took off down the road.

"What now?" Thomas wondered aloud. "When they come back it won't be a surprise. True, they don't know who we are or how many, but they have us outnumbered."

"What if we moved across to the other side of the road," Daniel suggested. "They have to be at least a mile down the road and that could give us several minutes."

"It's worth a try," Thomas agreed. "We sure can't take off an go anywhere, cause the wagons can't outrun them. Hurry up. Let's get the wagons and go."

The teams were driven hurriedly across the roadway and back into the underbrush and rocks as far as they could go. Then once more, the boys took branches and wiped out the tracks as best they could. The two reloaded their rifles and changed out the cylinder in the revolver, then carefully found the safest places they could with good views of the road and open ground between offering no protection to any who would attack. They made sure there were more protective rocks and brush behind them so that they had room to retreat a ways.

All was silence. They waited.

After several minutes the sound of racing horses approached from the east.

"They're back in those rocks," the wounded man shouted as he pointed the way.

"Let's go!" their leader ordered as he turned off the road and rode hard toward the rocks with his gun blazing.

The rest of the riders opened fire with him and there was a roar of gunfire as all charged to where the wagons and their drivers had been. But no one returned fire. There were no wagons. There were no drivers.

"Quick!" their leader called. "Up the road. They already have a lead on us!"

The outlaw band returned to the road and headed west at a full gallop. Moments later, all was silent once again.

* * *

Thomas holstered his revolver and motioned for Daniel to do the same. They stood for a moment and gazed out from their hiding place at the three men who lay in the dirt across the road and the horses that grazed quietly on the scrub grass near the bushes off to the side of the road.

"What should we do?" Daniel wondered.

"Don't know," Thomas replied. "They's sure to be up the road if we go on. They might even guess what we done and come on back again. We'll have to stay put for a spell."

"What if those three ain't all dead? Do we see if we can help them?" the colored youth asked.

"I figure if they ain't movin', we ain't movin' neither. Let's set a spell here where we are and wait to see what happens." Thomas turned toward the wagons. "Let's git somethin' ta eat."

He took one last look at the still forms in the dirt on the other side of the road, then picked up his rifles and turned to walk to the wagons. Daniel picked up his weapons and followed.

The boys paused to reload their weapons.

Rummaging through the camp supplies, Thomas found some hard biscuits and a canteen of water. Leaning against a wagon wheel he shared the food with his friend and the two ate in silence. Interrupted by the sound of returning horsemen, they picked up their weapons and moved once more into protective rocks and bushes and waited to see what would happen.

The sun had risen toward noon as the cloud of dust that enveloped the advancing horsemen rolled in from the west. It wasn't long before the riders became visible as they charged furiously down the roadway. Their leader raised an arm and signaled a halt. The band stopped and the dust began to settle.

"They have to be here someplace," their leader shouted. "If they ain't where they was at first then maybe they crossed to the other side."

Thomas and Daniel pulled back the hammers on the rifles and took aim on the lead riders.

"Charge!" he ordered.

The rifles spoke and the band's leader and another were blown backwards out of their saddles. As the remaining riders yelled and charged in their direction with guns blazing, the boys drew their revolvers and started to fire in steady, aimed sequence. Three more riders were quickly unhorsed.

"Head back fer the rocks," one called, and the remaining riders wheeled their horses around to cross back over the road and into the rocks where the wagons had originally been hidden.

"Reload," Thomas whispered. The empty cylinders were replaced and the rifles were reloaded.

"How long before they try again?" Daniel asked.

"Don't know." Thomas wiped the dust from his glasses. "Surprise is still on our side. They haven't seen us, so they can't know fer sure how many we is or how well we're armed. Take out yer loaded cylinder and keep it close, and reload the empty while we've got a few minutes. If they start to move switch out cylinders and be ready to fight."

For several minutes there was no movement while the outlaws decided on their next move. Meanwhile the two empty cylinders were reloaded and the boys waited for the next move from across the road. As they waited, a rabbit scurried from the brush beside the road several yards to the east.

"Someone's crossing," Daniel observed. "Should I move back and watch for whoever it is?"

"Yeh. You go quietly to the east and back a ways and I'll move over toward the west," Thomas instructed.

The two moved according to plan, then settled and watched and waited.

Thomas heard a single rifle shot to the right, then silence. Daniel found his man, he thought to himself. Then he was surprised by a new, rapidly approaching much larger cloud of dust from the west. More trouble he figured.

Moments passed, then the men across the road saw the dust cloud, too. Without warning, the remaining bandits broke from their hiding places and charged eastward down the road.

Daniel worked his way back to where they had separated. Thomas did the same. They stood in silence wondering what would be next. Soon the new riders were upon them, then passing eastward along the road, nearly two dozen poorly clad Confederate cavalrymen. As they passed, the last half dozen pulled out of the charge and stopped to investigate the bodies lying on either side of the roadway.

"What's happened here?" a young sergeant commented to his troopers as they glanced about. "There has to be something else we're not seeing."

"There is," Thomas spoke up stepping forward from his hiding place. He motioned for Daniel to remain hidden.

"Who are you?" the man asked. "and what are you doing here? And what happened here?"

The sergeant was clearly surprised and bewildered by what he saw -- five bodies dead or wounded and a single young boy.

"My name is Thomas Reynolds, Sergeant. My father runs freight service between Ozark, Arkansas, and the western and Indian territories. I'm on my way to deliver a shipment to Fort Wayne in Oklahoma Indian Territory. A band of men attacked my wagons and I had to defend myself."

"You have more than one wagon?" the sergeant asked.

"Two, Sir."

"And where are they? How many of you are driving them?"

"They're hidden in the rocks and scrub growth. And there's two of us."

The sergeant pushed his hat back in disbelief and scratched his head. For a moment he said no more as he stared at the boy and studied the possible truth of what he said. Thomas stood uneasy, wondering if this soldier could be trusted, or if he and his troopers might just decide to steal his wagons themselves.

"How is it that two boys stood off this band of outlaws and survived without a scratch and so many of them dead and wounded?"

Thomas glanced past the soldiers to see if any who had fallen were moving or if all might be dead. He saw there was some movement and that the other soldiers had gone to see what they might do.

"Cain't rightly say, Sir, other than some quick thinking and a lot of luck."

"I give you credit for spunk and determination. Where's your partner and let's see to these wagons and to getting you safely on your way."

"Give us a minute and Daniel and me will pull them around." Thomas turned and disappeared into the rocks and scrub to join Daniel and drive out the wagons.

There was the commotion of movement as the horses pushed through the brush and drew the wagons into the open.

"What are you doin' with a nigger, boy?" the man asked in surprise.

"My pa rented his services as his regular drivers is off fightin' fer the Confederacy." He reached into his pocket. "Here's the contract agreement." He showed the paper to the trooper.

"Guess it's all in order." He glanced over the agreement then handed the paper back to the boy. "You two best get on your way. We'll finish up here and take care of anyone we find on up the road." He put a caring hand on the boy's shoulder. "You be careful. These ain't the only bad ones on the road these days. We've been after this bunch for some time now. Soon's we're done here, we'll be headed back to Fort Wayne ourselves. Just know we'll be behind you. Jest how far, I don't know." He lifted his hat and pushed his hair back some. "But in case we don't meet again, good luck to you."

"Come on Daniel," Thomas instructed, "Let's be on our way."

The sergeant had turned to mount his horse, but stopped suddenly. "Yer awful familiar with this nigger boy. Be careful, there are lots who run away out here."

"Why shouldn't I be, we grew up together, and as has known each other all our lives."

"Oh," the man replied. "Get on your way then."

Thomas and Daniel slapped the reins and put their teams in motion. Moving west along the road, they glanced back only once to be sure the soldiers were as good as their word and did not follow behind. It was early afternoon as they left behind the scene of their recent combat, moving on in the heat of the day.

As the sun drifted down toward the horizon, it became evident that the wagons could not reach Fayetteville before dark. White wispy clouds began to appear in the sky. Before long they began to thicken, then rise into dark thunderheads.

"Should we find some place and pull off for the night?" Daniel asked.

"Yeh," Thomas responded. He shaded his eyes with his hand and glanced skyward. "We best find high ground," he quickly surveyed the landscape, then pointed to a higher rocky outcrop with space on the backside for the wagons, low scrub trees, nothing too high. "Over there seems safest. If there's lightning we don't want to be near the higher trees, and the rocks should provide a place to hide from the view of the road."

Turning his team off the road, Thomas led the way up a gentle slope to the rocks.

"Don't worry about tracks. It'll rain fer sher and we need to secure the horses where they will be safest and tie everything down against the wind."

The wagons were parked side by side with space in between to tie the horses on lines stretching between the wagons. They were fed grain from the wagons. The boys ate cold beans and biscuits, washing it down with water from their canteens. Making sure the wagon covers were tied down tightly, they set out their bedding in the wagon with their personal gear and settled in early for the night.

Before the sun set, it was blocked out by the gathering storm. The rumble of thunder began in the distant western hills and rolled in quickly with flashes of lightning in the far distance, but rushing closer quickly. Suddenly the storm was upon them with howling winds and blinding flashes of lightning and deafening crashes of thunder. It drove through blowing sheets of stinging rain with tiny bits of hail rattling on canvass and pounding like buckshot on the horses' hides. They danced in pain turning to face the storm with heads bowed down toward the ground to avoid as much of the storm's fury as possible.

Suddenly it was over. A broken moon glowed in the sky and a million bits of sparkling starlight danced across the black heavens. The night came alive with the chatter of insects and the distant mournful howl of coyotes. Placing their revolvers near the head of their bedding, the boys drifted off to sleep and the horses rested, sleeping where they stood.

The long day had ended, and all was well.

*   *   *

Bright sunlight streamed in through the opening in the back of the wagon, glaring across the sleeping faces in the wagon bed. Daniel opened his eyes and winced at the strong glare of the light. Putting his hand across his face, he sat up and turned his back on the brightness.

"Hey, Thomas," he shook his friend's shoulder. "It's morning."

Thomas stirred, covered his eyes against the bright sun, sat up, and reached in his boot for his glasses. Throwing off his blankets, he took his clothing from its folded pile used as a pillow, and dressed. Each boy rolled up his bedding and tied it into a roll, stowing it with the personal gear in the wagon bed.

"Let's cook up something hot," Thomas suggested. "It's cold out and I'm hungry."

"I like that idea," Daniel agreed as he pulled on his boots.

It was chilly as the two climbed down from the wagon, so they reached in for their dusters before setting out to collect firewood. Whatever they didn't use for their fire, they would stow in the slings beneath the wagons. A small fire was built between the wagons, the coffee pot was hung over the flame, and bacon was laid out in a pan. Each boy diced a potato and the bits were thrown in with the bacon. Biscuits were pulled from the supplies along with a can of beans. The lid was cut open and folded back and the beans were place in the coals near the edge of the fire. Eating utensils, tin plates and cups were taken out by Daniel while Thomas attended to the cooking. The two took a deep breath of the warm aroma of the cooking food and closed their eyes to enjoy the smell. It was nearly fifteen minutes before they filled their plates and cups then sat back against the wagon wheel to eat and enjoy the food and hot coffee.

There was no rush. They ate till all was gone, then drew water from the water keg on the side of the wagon to wash the dish ware. When all was packed away, each had a last cup of coffee. The pot was emptied on the remains of the fire, with a hiss and a cloud of steam. It and the cups were rinsed out. All was put away.

The teams were watered, then hitched to the wagons and all was made ready to continue to Fayetteville.

The long shadows of wagons and horses stretched before them in the low early morning sunlight as the wagons pulled onto the roadway and continued westward on their journey. It was a relief to begin the day without the choking road dust. The surface was still damp from the storm of the previous night and the heavy dew that followed. Some puddles remained in a few places where mud splattered as the horses' hoofs splashed their way through. Thomas pushed his glasses up on the bridge of his nose, took a firm grip on the reins, and allowed the team to walk at an easy pace as they began the day's journey. He expected that they would pull into Fayetteville by mid day where they would put up at Morgan's Freight Company for the rest of the day and give the teams a rest.

*   *   *

The layover at Morgan's was a great relief from the days on the road. First, the horses got a break and some good grain and water, not to mention a day without pulling wagons. The boys had a tasty home-cooked meal and real beds to sleep in. And the company and day off the road were relaxing. The water keg was emptied and refilled with fresh water. Food stores were resupplied with fresh food. Clothes were washed and the boys, too, had baths.

On the second morning after their arrival, Thomas and Daniel hitched up the teams, bade farewell, and began the journey to Bentonville. This would be the last day on a road. The two would spend the night with Sheriff Carleton at Bentonville, then head off cross country to Fort Wayne.

*　　*　　*

The final day of travel dawned misty and wet. The road out of Bentonville headed northwest toward Maysville. About twelve miles out, a rough wagon trail cut west along a branch of the Arkansas River toward Fort Wayne. About sixteen miles of rough terrain remained to the journey's end at the fort. It was mid day when the wagons turned west, away from the main road, to follow the rutted trail along the river.

"We're almost there," Daniel sighed as the two took a break at the river.

"Remember what Sheriff Carleton warned?" Thomas remarked. "There may be just a few miles left, but this area is very dangerous because it's close to the Missouri line and raiders run this area."

"The horses are rested from our recent stops," Daniel stated. "Should we make a run for it?"

Thomas took a drink from his canteen, pushed the stopper back in, and thought a moment before answering. "We'll not run, but will move more quickly. Put on your gun belt and keep the rifles loaded and ready in the wagon bed at your feet. Save the horses for a flat out run if we need it further on. I hope that if we do need to run, we'll be close enough to make it to the fort and safety." He pushed his glasses up and reached the canteen up to the wagon seat. "Let's get armed and move out."

The two armed themselves, checked the saddle horses in case they would be needed, then climbed up onto the wagon seats.

They slapped the reins and put their teams into an easy canter, running at a slow, steady pace without stressing the teams.

Three miles had passed when a small cloud of dust rose on the horizon to the north. Snapping the reins loudly, the horses were urged into a faster pace and began a race to gain as much distance as possible before the distant riders could close in on the wagons. The dust cloud quickly rose as the dust from the wagons rolled out behind, covering the second team and wagon with a fine tan-colored powder. Daniel coughed from breathing the dust and the horses tossed their heads, snorting their dislike for the discomfort of the choking dust. It stuck to sweating animals, irritated the eyes of animals and driver, covered wagon canvass and load, and stuffed up noses making it hard to breathe. The distant riders were closing steadily, approaching at an angle that would bring them in beside the wagons, to fire directly at their drivers. A fight would come soon.

Fifteen minutes passed. The boys could see the riders within their cloud of dust. The riders could see the boys. Flashes of light were quickly followed by the crack of gunfire. Bullets ripped the canvass and thumped into the wagon wood. But the first shots missed boys and animals. Thomas and Daniel felt helpless in their inability to fire back and drive the teams at the same time.

Thomas had an idea. He tied the reins in a knot and slipped them over his head and around his waist. Letting go, the boy waited to see if the horses would continue to run without having his hands on the lines. They ran on. Picking up a rifle, Thomas took careful aim at a lead rider, tried to allow for his movement and the bounce of the wagon, pointed to a spot just ahead of the rider, then squeezed the trigger. The rider dropped his weapon and slumped forward in his saddle. Lucky shot, he thought.

The remaining riders broke around the first and kept on coming. Daniel drew his revolver and fired six slow, but wild shots as he drove the team with one hand and attempted to point his gun with the other. The riders continued to fire back. Most shots went wild, but some continued to hit the wagons and two of the horses were grazed. Without warning, Daniel felt pain as a bullet ripped through his boot and tore the flesh in the calf of his leg. He dropped the revolver onto the seat boards and grabbed on to keep from falling off from the shock of the impact. He realized that he had to stop the bleeding or he would pass out from loss of blood.

Daniel noticed how Thomas had tied the horses reins and did the same. Then he ripped the cloth from the tail of his shirt and tied it tightly around his leg. It should hold, he thought.

The wagons continued to bounce wildly along the rough trail as the attackers attempted to move in closer. Trying again with another of his rifles, Thomas managed to hit another rider, causing him to fall and his horse to trip and go down. Another rider was knocked down by the falling horse. Moments later, Thomas was hit as a bullet passed clear through the palm of his left hand, which was outstretched, reaching for another rifle. He dropped the rifle and pulled back in pain.

A running battle had gone on for about fifteen minutes, but seemed more like an hour. A lead horse on Thomas's wagon was hit badly. Its life blood spewed forth into the air, splashing on the others and flying through the air hitting driver and wagon. Thomas pulled the team up before the horse would fall and bring the whole rig to a crashing halt. Daniel pulled his team across the front of Thomas's. The two jumped down and before the riders could react, pulled loose their saddled horses, jumped on and raced westward toward the fort. Knowing the wagons were going nowhere, the raiders raced on after the boys.

The chase continued on for another two miles when it became evident that the horses were tiring. But the bandits' horses were also tiring and the chase began to feel like slow motion. More shots were fired, but they went wild. Thomas and Daniel chose not to return fire, but to urge their horses on in the hope of reaching the safety of the fort. They rode their horses in a zig-zag pattern hoping to make it harder for the enemy to hit them. But it also tended to slow them down.

Another column of dust rose ahead of them on the road. Fearing the worse, Thomas watched for a place where they could pull off and take a stand. He noticed a stand of small scrubby trees to the left and motioned to Daniel. The boys swung sharply toward the trees, catching the riders by surprise once more. This allowed enough time to dismount behind the trees and pull their revolvers to fight back. Daniel had to reload his and quickly exchanged his empty cylinder for a loaded one out of his cartridge bag.

The riders turned to attack, but the boys were on solid ground and able to take careful and steady aim. Each fired three carefully measured rounds, taking down two approaching riders and wounding a third. The bandits pulled up and retreated for another attack. For the first time, the boys could count nearly two dozen raiders, still in the saddle, preparing to finish them off.

Suddenly, out of the approaching second column came the sound of a bugle and the thunder of charging troops. The column swung open into a wide pair of lines and opened fire on the riders preparing to finish off the boys. The bandits fell quickly and were soon overtaken by several dozen cavalry troopers in gray. The fighting ended in minutes and the two boys, each leading his horse, stepped forth from their cover in grateful surprise. But their surprise was even more intense when, upon closer look, they found their rescuers to be a troop of Indians.

The captain rode up to the boys. "What happened here? Who are you boys?" he asked

"Captain, these men attacked us on the road some miles back and tried to kill us and take our wagons," Thomas replied. "I'm Thomas Reynolds, running freight to Fort Wayne for my pa's freight company out of Ozark, Arkansas. This here's our rented help, Daniel. Our wagons are about a mile to the east with at least one dead horse in the traces. We could use some medical help." He pointed to Daniel's leg wound and held up his bleeding hand.

"I'm Captain Waters of the Cherokee mounted troops out of Fort Wayne," he introduced. "Corporal," the captain called to a nearby trooper, "get a medic to help these boys."

The soldier rushed off to find the troop's doctor.

"You're lucky we happened along," the captain continued. "Why don't you have any help, at least two to a wagon?"

The boy answered, "Most of the men have gone off to fight in the army. We really didn't know things was so bad out here." He winced in pain and, taking a bandana from his pocket, grabbed it with his hand and wrapped it to control the bleeding.

The corporal returned with the doctor. The captain motioned him to hurry.

"Let's have a look," he offered. "You boys have a seat on this tree trunk, he indicated a large trunk lying on the ground that had fallen in some previous storm. "The hand is broken. We'll have to wrap it with a slab of wood so it can mend." He turned to examine Daniel's leg wound. "You were smart to wrap it so tightly. The bullet tore away a chunk of flesh and you could have bled dangerously, maybe even died. But the wound itself is not seriously bad. When we get you two back to the fort, we'll make a poultice for each to draw out infection and you will both heal fine. Just now we'll wrap the wounds then get on our way."

The doctor put a clean bandage on each wound.

"Now, Captain, we need to get these two and their wagons on the way and back to the fort."

The boys mounted their horses and turned toward the road, keeping close by each other as they headed back to the east to check on the wagons and move them on to the fort.

"I sure am glad these guys came along," Daniel whispered. "I don't think we'd have survived another charge. How's your hand?"

"Hand hurts like hell," Thomas whispered back. "How's your leg? And yer right. They'd have finished us fer sure." He pushed his glasses back up on his nose and took a firm grip of the reins with his right hand.

*   *   *

The sun was well passed noon by the time the wagons were back on the road. The dead horse had been removed from the harness and the gear removed and stowed in the wagon. Some of the Cheyenne troopers skinned and field butchered the carcass and wrapped the meat in wagon canvas to be taken back for the women to prepare and smoke for future use. The doctor checked the horses' wounds and put salve on those that needed. Thomas's team was rearranged so that the lone horse was in front and two were in back. The wagons were underway within the hour with a full cavalry escort. One company of troopers was assigned to finish rounding up the remaining raiders to be arrested and taken to the fort. Those dead were stripped of weapons and any useful clothing and left to the buzzards.

By late afternoon, all had arrived at Fort Wayne. The horses were turned loose in the corral. The wagons were parked near the trading post. The boys were given quarters in a storeroom in the back of the store. With medical needs attended, they went with the soldiers to the mess hall where they were treated with honored respect and shared the story of their journey with many who wanted to know.

*   *   *

Runs Like the Wind stood over six feet in height with long black hair tied in rawhide laces. Sun-darkened skin was firm and muscular with the strength of constant activity from the hunt and from military patrols. He sat by a low fire outside his tepee dwelling and listened as Daniel and Thomas told of their journey. He had already received the blanket, seen the note, and placed the paper on the burning coals of the fire. The three were seated on the ground, enjoying the privacy of no one else about to interrupt with questions or listen to a conversation they wished to keep to themselves.

"I thought we were done for sure," Daniel said softly. "There were way too many of them, and one last charge without stopping was all they needed. I'm so glad the patrol was in the area."

"I know you boys have a room in the store. But you might want to sleep with your wagons so things don't walk away during the night. I will bring my son and we will camp with you. I will also bring our dog to wake us if anyone comes around. Then we will help you unload tomorrow."

"Thank you, Sir," Thomas acknowledged. "We've had enough trouble. I just want to get everything where it's to go, get rested, and start back again. I jest might take my pa's suggestion and leave the wagons. With just the two saddle horses and as little gear as needed, I hope to get home a lot faster than it took to get here."

"You two go make camp. Little Falcon and I will be along shortly with the dog. Tomorrow, we will set your camp by my tepee and put all your gear there and tie your horses with my ponies. We'll unload the wagons and arrange things with the horses, wagons, and gear, and get your payment for your pa. Then you will be finished with your job and free to spend time as we wish."

Runs Like the Wind stood to go into his tepee and gather his son, dog, and gear to camp the night with Thomas and Daniel. The boys stood, stretched, then turned toward the wagons to prepare a campfire for the night, using wood from the harness beneath the wagon.

*   *   *

Business was concluded during the following day. Payment of $500 in Confederate currency was made for all. Gold was offered, being more easily available this far west, but the weight would be too much to carry safely without risking loss should a fast getaway be needed. The warrior's wife, Desert Flower, suggested sewing the money into the underside of the saddle for safekeeping and offered to do so. It was done and the saddle was kept inside the warrior's tepee to avoid loss.

April slipped into May. Thomas, Daniel, and Little Falcon had become good friends as they hunted and fished together, hiked off to explore the countryside, and took an occasional opportunity to go swimming in the nearby river.

One night during the first week of May, all were seated around the campfire, enjoying the song of the wild creatures and a warm cup of coffee, thinking back over recent events, and wondering what might be next. Runs Like the Wind spoke up.

"Thomas, some years ago we met when your pa was out here for a delivery. I knew then that you might grow into a strong and worthy warrior and offered your pa the opportunity for you to take your vision quest and become a warrior of the tribe. You would not be expected to stay, but would always be welcome to join with us whenever possible.

"Do you wish it?"

Thomas paused as he thought about it. His glasses had again slipped down on the bridge of his nose and he automatically pushed them back up with the back of his hand. He knew the question might come up from what his pa had said before they left on their journey. But he had no way of understanding what it meant.

"Sir," the boy replied, "I am honored that you would ask. But I don't understand what it is that you ask. I know so little about your people, your history, your customs. I would like to know. I would like to say yes."

The warrior sipped from his cup, then set it aside on the ground.

"My people," he began, "hold the earth as our mother. Its creatures are the helper spirits of the Great Spirit, the same as your God. We take our names from those spirits. When we are born, our parents give us our childhood names. But when we grow to the age you boys are now, we go in search of our helper spirits from the world of living creatures and natural life. We seek a vision in which we will learn of that spirit and from that we take our grown up name. Each child in his own turn goes on a quest to seek a vision and learn which spirit helper will be his guide in life and to learn the name he will use as a man. This we call the vision quest." The man paused to drink from his cup and to study the boy for a moment.

"We often begin the quest by bathing and going to the sweat lodge to clean and purify the body," he continued. "You will then be taken to a remote area where you will stay for a few days, fasting, meditating, and praying. During that time, at the end of each day, someone will bring a little food and water and make sure you are okay. Before you return, you will probably have your dream and learn of your spirit helper and your new name. When all the boys who have gone on their vision quests return, there is a ceremony where each tells his story in dance and takes his new name. I will sponsor you in all this. Littler Falcon is old enough for his vision quest and Daniel, by his age and his bravery in the events of your journey has earned the right to go on his vision quest as well.

"Now do you think you are ready?"

"Runs Like the Wind, I am ready for my vision quest," Thomas stated.

"Thank you," Daniel joined in. "I am honored to be allowed to join and would like very much to go on my vision quest."

"I will talk of this with the others and find out when the council determines the next vision quest to be held.

"Now, if you boys wish, you and the dog can sleep out here by the fire tonight." The warrior stood. "Desert Flower and I will say good night. It's getting late."

Runs Like the Wind and his squaw stood and left for their tepee. Little Falcon reached out and put some small pieces of wood into the fire.

"You get your blankets and I'll get mine?" he asked.

"Okay," both chorused in unison. "Be right back." Daniel stated.

The sky had turned a velvet black with a million sparkling pieces of starlight. Without a word, the three brought their blankets and spread them on the ground near the firelight. All around the insects of the night chirped their noisy songs and in the distance, the coyotes howled. There was a peace in the air, a sense of security, a feeling that on this night, all was well in this one place in the vicinity of Fort Wayne.

*   *   *

The council met the next week and a time was chosen for the boys in the tribe to go on their vision quests. The moon would be full in another six days and that would be the night to be out in the wilderness. On the day before, the boys would strip off their clothes, bath in the river, and go to their sweat lodges where they would spend most of the day into the afternoon. Late in the day, the day before the full moon, they would dress in a breechclout and moccasins, their sponsors would take them into the hills to preselected locations, and they would prepare their separate camps where they would stay until each had his spirit dream. On the day of the full moon, they would awake, already at their dream sites.

In the early morning light and the long shadows of the new day, Little Falcon, Daniel, and Thomas all met at the river together with Runs Like the Wind. They took off their clothing and piled it on the river bank and walked into the cold water. The warrior was unflinching, but the boys shivered in the icy cold as the water deepened and rose up their bodies. Once knee deep in the river, each sat down and washed, splashing water in his face, across his shoulders, and over his head. They sat for several minutes as their bodies became accustomed to the cold and began to feel warm again. Then, rising to their feet, all walked to the shore, gathered their clothes, and walked naked back to the sweat lodge erected near their camp, and entered, leaving the clothing outside.

Inside the lodge, each was seated on an elk hide on the ground as water was sprinkled on rocks, heated by a low fire. The steam filled the air with a hot moist cloud bringing out a hot sweat which ran down the body and pooled on the ground. Wet sweat-soaked hair was plastered to head and neck and back. There they all sat for several hours. Nothing was said. No words were spoken from the time the day began other than "it is time" when the boys were first awakened.

Finally, in the later part of the afternoon, Little Falcon's father stood and signaled it was time to move on. The four left the lodge and stepped outside where they put on their breechclout and moccasins and prepared for the journey into the hills. The small group walked into the hills outside the area of the fort and its surrounding camps. Each boy in turn was given a camp site where his blankets had already been gathered along with a small fire and a supply of wood.

Thomas found himself out of sight of the others in the small clearing overlooking the fort below, surrounded by rocks, grass, some small trees and underbrush. Here he would stay until he had his vision.

*   *   *

In the days that followed, Runs Like the Wind made the rounds to visit each boy, bring a small piece of dried meat and a gourd of water, and talk briefly to be sure each was okay. Each night the boys would crawl beneath their blankets; listen to the sounds of the night creatures -- the insects, the owls, the mice, the coyotes; and shiver in the cold. During the day there was little to do but watch the world at a distance in miniature far below, and observe the wild life in the space nearby -- insects, birds, small animals such as rabbits. Nearby critters were not afraid of the boys. They sensed that each had become a part of the little world in which he was camped. The boys in turn became more observant of their living surroundings, having never before taken the time to notice. Now they had nothing but time.

Thomas was fascinated by the ants -- how small they were and how much they were involved in moving things to their little holes in the earth. Small birds were busy picking up scraps of grasses and twigs to build or repair their nests. He noticed a rabbit that came out of the same bushes each day, went about finding the tastyist grasses, nibbled, then returned to his nest. Elk and deer and buffalo grazed in the distance as they passed in small herds. But the most fascinating creature of all was the falcon. He would come floating high in the air, hovering as he watched the ground below in search of food, then swoop low and fast to snatch up some unsuspecting mouse and fly off with his prize to devour it in some distant place. After the second day, the dreams began. At first they were of his pa and home and life on the Ozark Queen. He dreamed of the trip he'd just made, the dangers, the quiet moments, and nearly loosing his life.

Then came the strangest dream of all. He and Daniel were running for their lives from the raiders. But they weren't driving wagons or riding horses. They were running. They had no weapons. They had no shoes. They had no clothes, only their long johns. They had just gotten up and crawled out of their blankets when the raiders attacked. Strange, too, the raiders were on foot. They were chasing them with sticks.

Then the strangest thing happened. Thomas heard a raucous calling in the sky. He looked up and saw the falcon that had flown above his vision camp. He knew it was the same, but did not know how. The bird swooped down and brushed the hats of the running raiders, knocking one off. The men swung at it with their sticks, but kept on chasing. The Falcon rose high in the sky and called out again. Suddenly, from nowhere, there was a gathering of dozens of birds. Their numbers blackened the sky and blocked out the sunlight. The boys tripped and fell and Thomas noticed they weren't just two. Little Falcon was with them. He stood up and raised his hands to the sky. The birds rose as one mighty cloud, then dove down, grabbing the sticks out of the hands of the raiders and slicing their scalps with their sharp talons. The men turned and fled. The birds vanished and the sun shown brightly. The boys sat and looked at each other. It was over and Thomas awoke from his dream.

*   *   *

Five days after the cold bath and the sweat lodge, all were gathered once more around the fire before the warrior's lodge and the boys' camp. Each had had his vision. It was time to learn their meanings. Daniel was on a hunt, working his way through a heard of buffalo when he fell and would have been trampled. But a great white buffalo stood between him and the rest of the animals and they simply ran around him. His name became Standing Buffalo. The buffalo spirit would be his protector. Little Falcon became Swift Eagle, having dreamed of a race he ran with the eagle, to carry an important message to his people. He was faster than the eagle and got the message to his people in time to warn them of an attack. The eagle had not been slow, but had been shot by an enemy warrior. Wounded, he arrived later and was healed by Little Falcon and gave the boy his name. The falcon spirit became Thomas's protector and he became known simply as Falcon.

"The vision quest has been good for each of you," Runs Like the Wind concluded. "Each of you has learned your spirit helper and each has his second name. Desert Flower is working with new skins to make you each new cloths. I will work with you to make your medicine bags for your spirit helpers. They will be kept close to you as you wear them around your neck like the first medicine bag that Little Falcon wears."

The evening wore on and the fire was allowed to dwindle to coals. Soon they winked and grew dim as they vanished into the hot ash of the fire's wood.

"The night is here," Desert Flower spoke. "It has been a tiring time and we all need our sleep. Tomorrow will be a good day to begin your new lives. Now it is time for sleep."

"Tonight, go to your tents," the warrior instructed. "You all need a good night's sleep. Tomorrow we must plan for your futures."

Daniel poked at the fire with a lone stick. The coals glowed dimly as the dusty ash sent a light cloud into the air. It settled, covering the glow. The odor of the fire scented the air lightly. A broken moon cast its light on the camp. All turned to their tents and settled for the night.

*   *   *

In the days ahead several decisions were made. Runs Like the Wind and Desert Flower decided to keep Daniel, now know as Standing Buffalo, as a brother to Little Falcon, now know as Swift Eagle. They put their case to the council, citing Daniel's bravery during the journey from Ozark, his status as friend to Thomas and to his pa who had long been an honored friend of the Cherokee, and his current location in the Indian Territories, owing no allegiance to any laws of the states. The petition to adopt was granted.

It was now time to plan Thomas's safe return to his pa back in Ozark.

Desert Flower finished the new clothes. The warrior and the boys finished the medicine bags. There was a photographer at the fort who worked out of the trading post. Each of the boys would have his picture taken and copies would be made to share with each other.

The days passed without notice and May was passing to its new moon and the blackest night. Travel would be difficult and dangerous if the nights were too dark to see by. Therefore, Falcon would wait another seven days before heading back east. Because of the dangers on the trail between Fort Wayne and Bentonville, Runs Like the Wind asked if he, his boys, and a patrol of mounted rifles could travel with Falcon and patrol the trails for bandits as far as Bentonville. The patrol was approved. The fort commander was impressed by the bravery of the boys and the safe delivery of the supplies they had brought. The soldiers who had rescued them asked for the honor to ride with the party and patrol the country along the way.

*   *   *

On the twenty-first day of May, in the year 1862, a nighttime ceremony was held to honor the brave boys who had brought supplies to the fort. A great feast was shared. A large fire was lit. Dances of skill and celebration were shared, with events going late into the night. Loud drums and chants echoed into the darkness. A broken moon and a million specks of light cast a warm glow over the landscape. In the wee hours of the new day, all were tired and had gone to sleep. Many lay about the grounds surrounding the ceremonial fire. The fire itself had fallen to hot coals with showers of sparks rising into the air each time another log burned through and fell into the hot ashes. Swift Eagle's family slipped away to their camp and sat about their own small fire and talked of Falcon's return to the world of Thomas with the dawn of another day. This day would be a time for planning, resting from festivities, and packing for the journey.

As the day passed, Thomas's gear was sorted and packed into bundles tied in buffalo hides, designed to be hung from the saddle on Daniel's saddle horse. Weapons were cleaned and loaded. Captain Waters of the cavalry patrol provided four rifle boots, two for each saddle. The loaded rifles were stowed in the sleeves, ready for action when needed. Thomas would pack his own clothes and wear those of Falcon for the journey home. He was very proud of this gift from Desert Flower and wanted to show them off. Food stores and canteens were packed for easy access. If all went well, there would be one stop between the fort and Bentonville, and one stop between St. Paul and Fayetteville. Without wagons, the trip should be much quicker and hopefully, much safer.

On the second morning after the ceremonial evening, the sun rose, casting its light within the tent shared by Falcon and Standing Buffalo. Rays of bright light danced on the sleeping form of a third boy, Swift Eagle. The three had spent the last night together. The warrior's son stirred. Rubbing his eyes against the bright light, he sat up and glanced about at the others, still asleep, wrapped snugly in their blankets.

"Falcon, Standing Buffalo," he liked the sound of the new names. "The new day is here. It's a good day for a journey."

The other two rolled over and stared at the brightness of the low rays of the sun, reaching deep within the tent.

"Yeh, Swift Eagle," Falcon responded. "It does look like a good day. At least we'll be together for the first part of the journey. I do not wish to say good bye. But I sure can't wait to see my pa again. He must be worried. I've been gone for so long."

"It has been a long time," Standing Buffalo added. "But I like our new names."

"Shall we get this day going?" Swift Eagle asked.

"Yeh. Come on," Falcon agreed.

Crawling out of their blankets they shivered in the cold as they wore nothing but their breechclouts. Quickly they pulled on their leggings, tied them, pulled on their shirts, then slipped into their moccasins. The blankets were folded, rolled, and tied. All else had already been packed and prepared for the trip.

Stepping out of the tent into the morning light, they smelled the aroma of food as Desert Flower prepared a fresh stew of cut up elk meat and beans. A bread was baking on a stick. A sassafras tea was brewing in a clay pot. Runs Like the Wind was already about preparing the packs for the extra horse and gathering saddles and gear to be ready to load when the food had been eaten and final preparations were to be completed. In the distance, a bugle sounded within the fort as the troops gathered for morning colors and their orders for the day. Those traveling with the eastbound party would break for breakfast, then load their supply wagon and move to Runs Like the Wind's campsite in the camp outside the fort.

Within the small campsite, the food was consumed, tent and gear packed, horses loaded, and final farewells exchanged.

"Falcon, you be careful," Desert Flower admonished. "Swift Eagle, you bring your father and your brother home safely." She hugged her son, then her husband and adoptive son in turn. Finally she turned once more to Falcon. "I'll miss you, Falcon." She reached out and hugged him, too. "You tell your father what has happened here and that we have taken Standing Buffalo as our son. He is honored and loved by his new family."

"I will, Desert Flower. I'll miss you all, too. I cannot forget you because I wear the clothes you made for me. They will remind me, too, of all that we have shared in our time together. Pa will be honored by all I tell him. Maybe, after this war is over, we will return to see how you are. Maybe you all can come and visit us in Ozark. Now I am glad to have two more days with friends as I begin my journey home."

"It's a good day for a journey," the warrior said. At a sound from the fort, he looked up and said, "The soldiers are coming. We must leave now."

They mounted their horses and waved at the woman standing by the tepee. She waved back. The small party turned their horses to join the cavalry patrol. As the woman watched, her family with Falcon and the mounted soldier patrol headed east on the wilderness trail. For the next fifteen minutes she stood and watched as the group shrank into the distance, disappeared in the cloud of their trail dust, then the dust itself, drifted into nothing.

*   *   *

Six days later, a tired and dusty Indian boy, leading a pack horse and an extra saddle horse, rode down the busy streets of Ozark. Few took notice as he worked his way through the busy traffic of the streets. But the man outside the Reynolds Freight Company office stopped sweeping the front walkway as he looked up and recognized the boy on the lead horse. He set the broom against the front doorway and stepped off the wooden walk into the street. There he waited with hands on hips and a heart filled with pride.

His son was home.

About the author
J. Arthur Moore

J. Arthur Moore is an educator with 42 years experience in public, private, and independent settings. He is also an amateur photographer and has illustrated his works with his own photographs. In addition to **West to Freedom** Mr. Moore has written **Journey into Darkness**, a story in four parts, **Blake's Story, Revenge and Forgiveness**, two Civil War historic fictions, **Summer of Two Worlds**, a Native American historic fiction set in Montana Territory in the summer of 1882. This third Civil War era historic fiction, **West to Freedom**, is the first new release in six years. While the setting for the story, the Cherokee nation as a part of the Confederacy, and the historic places are real, the story itself is purely a work of fiction.

A graduate of Jenkintown High School, just outside of Philadelphia, Pennsylvania, Moore attended West Chester State

College, currently West Chester University. Upon graduation, he joined the Navy and was stationed in Norfolk, Virginia, where he met his wife to be, a widow with four children. Once discharged from the service, he moved to Coatesville, Pennsylvania, began his teaching career, married and brought his new family to live in a 300-year-old farm house in which the children grew up and married, went their own ways, raised their families to become grandparents themselves.

Retiring after a 42-year career, Mr. Moore has moved to the farming country in Lancaster County, Pennsylvania, where he plans to enjoy the generations of family, time with his model railroad, and time to guide his writings into a new life through publication. It also allows for the opportunity to participate in a local model railroad club as well as time for traveling to Civil War events, and presenting at various organizations and events about the boys who were part of that war. He also shares the process of writing, and readings from his work, and does book signings at a variety of locations.

Mr. Moore can be reached through the contact page of the website for his books at **www.jarthurmoore.com** with links to his Facebook and Twitter pages; and a boys page focusing on the stories of the boys who served in the Civil War.

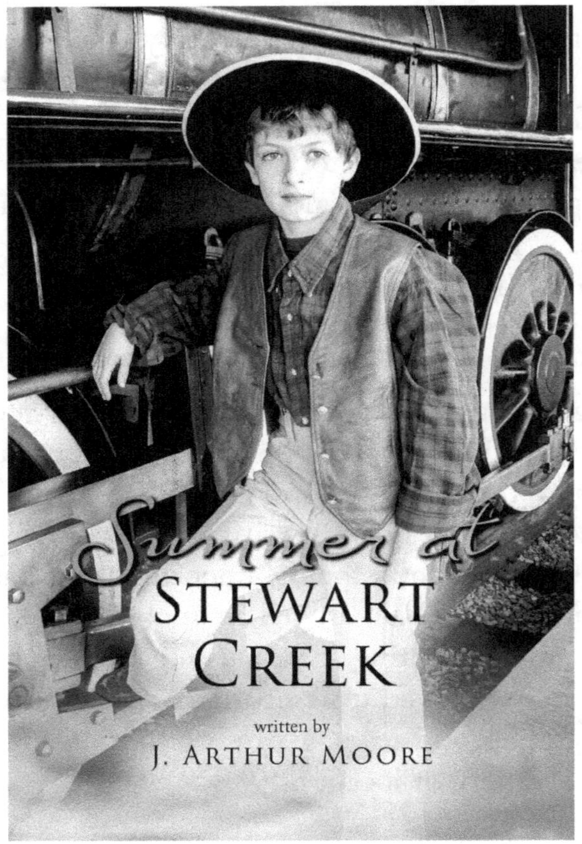

PREVIEW

Another new release in time for the Christmas holidays,
totally unlike any previous work by this author

Coming in time for the Christmas holiday season 2020. **Summer at Stewart Creek** is a unique fiction. Unlike everything J. Arthur Moore has published to date, this fiction is just fiction. Set in the land of the Virginia & Truckee Railroad of West Virginia, it is a family's story of new challenges in a new and unfamiliar town. Brett Tompkins leaves his home in Baltimore to spend his twelfth summer with his father in a logging town named Snow

Shoe, West Virginia. His father, a banker by trade, has taken over the family logging company at the request of Brett's grandfather who is no longer able to operate it due to failing health. But mother is not happy with this and gives him only a year to try it out. Reluctantly, she allows her son to spend the summer with his father at Snow Shoe. During the summer of 1879, Brett meets new friends and new adventure at Stewart Creek Logging Company, and comes to enjoy life in the mountain country. But can he convince his mother, a city woman, to visit and, hopefully, feel the same joy for the mountain country that he had come to feel.

The story's setting is recreated in miniature on the author's model railroad and the book is illustrated with photos from the railroad in miniature. Due to these photos, the book will be published in color only at $15.00 paperback, $25.00 hardback, and $3.99 eBook. It will become available for purchase as soon as its information is uploaded on the website, www.jarthurmoore.com, by the beginning of November 2020.